P9-AGW-841

Sleeping Beauty Wakes

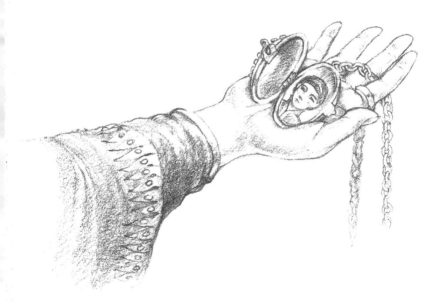

M.C. Hall

Illustrated by Judith A. Mitchell

Rigby

Contents

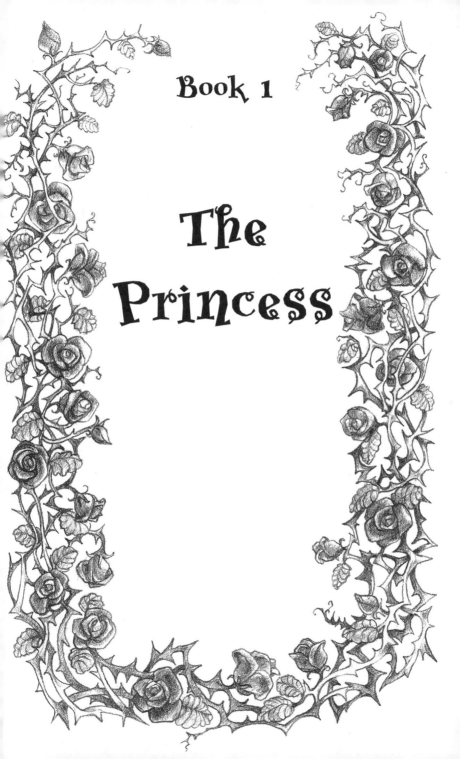

Book 1

The Princess

1

The Wish

Once upon a time, many hundreds of years ago, there lived a handsome king and his beautiful queen. Together, they ruled with kindness and grace over the lovely kingdom of Cambria.

Though not considered wealthy or powerful, Cambria was rich in the qualities that truly matter. It was a peaceful and happy land. The king and queen, and their two small sons, were admired and loved by their subjects. However, there was one thing the kingdom lacked— a princess.

"I would dearly love to have a daughter," sighed King Walter one day. He flinched as his sons, Hugh and William, darted past the throne. The young princes were dueling with wooden swords and shouting at one another. All of which was typical behavior for the high-spirited boys.

"Yes," agreed Queen Winifred. "I love our sons more than life itself. Still, it would be pleasant to have a little girl as well. A quiet and gentle child who would never knock over a suit of armor or upset her nurse by putting a frog in a water goblet."

"A child who could grow to be a comfort to us in our old age," added the king. "Who would be content to sit quietly beside us and listen to our stories of Cambria's past."

"Someone who would happily join me in the garden for embroidery lessons," said the queen. How she longed for a daughter who shared her fondness for needlework and other ladylike pursuits.

"But wishing will not make it so, my dear," said the king. "After all, no girl has been born to my family for centuries. It seems unlikely that one ever will."

"Highly unlikely," agreed Queen Winifred, shaking her head sadly. She sighed as the princes ran past again, their once-clean doublets now torn and dirty.

2

Briar Rose

Sometimes even the most unlikely wishes have a way of coming true. Barely a year later, King Walter and Queen Winifred stood gazing down at the royal cradle. Inside, a tiny bundle lay wrapped in a blanket of rose-colored silk.

"She is so beautiful," breathed the queen. "Isn't she beautiful, Walter?"

"As lovely as her mother," said the king, who was completely entranced by his daughter. And with good reason: the child *was* lovely, with rosy cheeks, dark curls, and eyes the blue of the brightest summer sky. The princess was more than beautiful, however. She was also a happy baby who rarely cried. Her very presence seemed to bring joy to those around her.

"We shall name her Briar Rose," announced the queen. "For my favorite flower."

"As you wish, my dear," said the king. "And we will give a marvelous feast to celebrate her naming day."

So the guest list was drawn up. Everyone who was anyone was invited—kings and queens, dukes and duchesses, lords and ladies. And, of course, the Wise Women of the forest.

"We must invite them," said the queen. "They will bring good fortune to our daughter."

"The Wise Women are always honored and welcomed guests," said the king. "But only 12 of them, Winifred. I refuse to allow Cassandra into the castle. She may be wise, but she is also cruel."

"Yes, dear," murmured the queen. She well remembered Cassandra, who had almost ruined Prince William's naming day, four years earlier. The unpleasant woman had put a curse on a young lord who annoyed her slightly, turning him into a particularly ugly toad. It had been months before the gentleman was himself again. The queen had since heard disturbing stories of other evildoings—even more serious—on Cassandra's part. The woman would never again be invited to share in one of Cambria's celebrations.

By the time the great day arrived, the king and queen had forgotten all about Cassandra. The morning dawned clear and warm, with sunshine seeking out even the gloomiest corners of the great castle. From king and queen to serving maid and groom, everyone donned his or her best clothing. For once, even Prince Hugh and Prince William looked clean and neat.

"Not that your fine appearance will last for long,"

muttered Effie, their nurse. She tugged at the hem of Hugh's doublet.

"It's fine, Effie," protested Hugh. "Leave it alone. You're only going to rip it if you keep pulling like that."

"Mind your manners," said the nurse sharply. "You know that your mother wants you both to be presentable for your baby sister's naming-day celebration."

"We *are* presentable, Effie. Now can we please go out to the courtyard and watch the guests arrive?"

"Yes, can we?" echoed William.

Effie stared at the two freckle-faced princes sternly, then sighed and gave in. "Along with you then," she said. "But keep out of the way. And don't go near the stables, you hear? I won't have you getting dirty!"

Before she had finished her list of dos and don'ts, the boys were out the door. In their mad dash, they nearly collided with their mother, who was entering with Briar Rose.

Still shaking her head at the boys' excitement, Effie took the baby into her arms. "At least this one I can dress to my satisfaction," she said. She set to work, outfitting the baby in a dress of the finest white linen and brushing her soft, dark curls.

"Oh, just look at her, Effie," said the proud queen.

"She's every inch the princess, Your Majesty."

Just then a bell began to toll loudly. "The celebration is about to begin!" cried the queen.

"Then we'd best get the guest of honor where she belongs," replied Effie. Carrying Briar Rose, she followed the queen down the stairs and into the great hall.

By the time the women arrived, a crowd of well-wishers already filled the huge room. The queen quickly took her place beside her husband. She checked to see that Hugh and William were safely in their seats, one at each side of their parents.

Effie carefully placed the princess in a lace-trimmed cradle near her family. The baby lay there, gurgling happily and smiling at the parade of faces that peered at her in admiration.

As soon as the guests had finished paying their respects, King Walter rose to his feet. "I have an important proclamation to make," he announced. "From this day forward, this castle and the land surrounding it belong to the princess and her female descendants."

A cheer rose from the crowd. It was unusual for property to be handed down on the female side. However, it was hardly unexpected for this king to make such a generous gesture. He had already announced his plans to divide the kingdom and its castles evenly among his children. Now he was making it clear that his daughter was assured of a fair share.

Then the feasting began. Platters of meat and fish disappeared as fast as they were carried into the banquet hall. So did trays of cakes, puddings, and other sweets.

Minstrels roamed the room, singing songs in honor of the princess. A colorful jester entertained the guests with his tricks. Hugh and William were soon close on his heels, considering him by far the most interesting adult in the room.

At last the feasting was done and it was time for the guests to present their gifts. All the usual items were given. There were tiny gowns of silk and velvet and slippers strewn with seed pearls. There was a peacock-feather fan and a miniature rocking chair crafted from rare woods. The princess even received her very own wooden sword, carved in secret by her brothers.

As was the custom, the Wise Women were the last to come forward with their offerings. Esmeralda, the eldest, approached the cradle first. "You shall grow more lovely each day," she said gently. The other guests murmured their approval.

Esmeralda was followed by her sister, Amanda. "Briar Rose, I give you the gift of intelligence," she said.

And so it went. One at a time, the Wise Women gifted the princess with kindness, humor, bravery, curiosity, and more. She was given everything in the world that she could want for a full and happy life.

The last of the Wise Women had just stepped toward the cradle when a harsh voice pierced the air. "So you think you can ignore me, do you?"

3

Cassandra's Curse

Horrified, the king and queen and their guests turned toward the doorway. A tall, bony figure stood there, dressed in black robes shot through with threads of gold. Wild black hair snaked its way down the woman's back, seeming to have a life of its own.

"Cassandra!" cried the queen. "But you were not invited."

"No, Your Highness, I was not," sneered Cassandra as she slowly entered the room. "And you will regret that omission—every one of you. But none so much as the fair princess." Now she looked down into the face of the babe, whose smile had vanished like the sun on a cloudy day.

"Here is your gift, child," Cassandra announced with an evil smile. "Before you turn 16, you will prick your finger on a spindle—and you will die!"

A collective gasp of horror came from the guests. And, as if she could understand, the baby started to wail.

Cassandra laughed wildly and began to spin. A gray

mist swirled around her, hiding her features. Then she disappeared from sight.

The queen darted forward and snatched Briar Rose from the cradle. Grasping the baby tightly in her arms, she turned to her stunned husband. "Do something, Walter! Send the guards after her!"

However, before the king could issue such an order, a bell-like voice spoke. "Wait, Your Majesty! I have not yet presented my gift."

It was Miranda, smallest and fairest of the Wise Women. She looked apologetically at the royal couple. "I had planned to give the princess the gift of obedience," she said. "A gift that I am sure you would have found most helpful. However, being obedient is not as important as being alive. I cannot undo my sister's curse, you understand. But I *can* attempt to soften it."

The king and queen stared at Miranda numbly, hardly taking in her words. However, when she reached out her arms, the queen hesitated for just a moment. Then she nodded slightly and handed her child to the Wise Woman.

The baby grasped one of Miranda's fingers and smiled. "You shall not die, Briar Rose," the woman said softly. "Instead you shall fall into a long and deep sleep. A sleep of 100 years."

There were a few appreciative murmurs from the crowd, along with low rumbles of distress. "One hundred years! But that is the same as death!"

"Not quite the same," said Miranda, addressing her response to the king and queen. "After all, sleeping means perchance waking again. Part of my gift is a promise of that possibility."

The king interrupted the confused murmurs that greeted this statement. "Thank you, Miranda," he said, taking his daughter into his arms. "We are grateful for your kindness. However, I will take things one step further. I will see to it that Cassandra's curse can never be fulfilled."

Holding Briar Rose, he turned to face his guests. "Beginning this very moment," he proclaimed, "all spinning wheels and spindles are banished from the kingdom.

"And furthermore," King Walter added, "no one shall ever speak to the princess of Cassandra's curse. I will not have her growing up in fear."

He looked down at his tiny daughter and smiled. "Nothing will ever harm you, Briar Rose. I give you my word."

4
Almost 16

"**H**ow long will you be gone, Hugh?"

"Not long, Rose," said Prince Hugh, looking fondly at his 15-year-old sister. "William and I'll be back before you can miss us."

"That would be impossible," said the princess. "You haven't left yet, and I already miss you."

William laughed. "Be honest. What you'll miss is a chance to get out of the castle without Mother and Father."

"Well, that *is* part of it," admitted Briar Rose. "When we're riding, *you* don't tell me to slow down and be careful. Besides, I love to hunt with you. I don't understand why this time they say I can't go. But no matter how prettily I ask, or how much I sulk, they refuse to change their minds."

Over their sister's head, William and Hugh exchanged a glance. "They have their reasons," said William. "And I think you should do as they say this time."

"You make it sound like I never listen to them," protested Briar Rose.

"Well . . ." began Hugh.

"Maybe it *is* time to act a bit more like a lady," William interrupted. "After all, you are almost 16."

The princess gave her brothers a hurt look. They were being unfair, she thought. The princes usually welcomed her into their ranks. They had encouraged her to tuck up her skirts and ride like the wind alongside them. They had taught her to shoot an arrow through a hoop from 50 yards and to track a deer through the forest. So why were they suddenly full of talk of ladylike behavior?

"We truly won't be gone long," said Hugh.

"So stop pouting and give us a kiss for luck," added William.

"Very well," said Briar Rose. "Without me along, you'll need it." She kissed each brother on the cheek. Then she stood and watched as they rode away.

However, Briar Rose was not about to forget her frustration at being left behind. "It's just not fair," she muttered to Effie later.

Effie had heard this complaint many times about many matters. So now she merely commented, "Your parents have your welfare at heart. As always."

"Pooh!" retorted Briar Rose. "My brothers are allowed to roam the countryside while I am expected to sit here in the castle. What harm could it possibly do to let me go with them? After all, they're not leaving Cambria. So it's not like I'd actually be going anywhere exciting. I never do."

"Your time will come, love," said Effie mildly.

"When? I'll be 16 in just a few days. Practically a woman. Yet I have never left Cambria! Never!"

"Well, the kingdom *is* very large, Briar Rose."

"That's not the point, Effie. I want to go places I've never been before. I want to see things I've never seen before. And do things I've never done before. I want—I want an adventure!"

Briar Rose's footsteps had quickened to match the torrent of words. So poor Effie had a hard time keeping up. "Your parents protect you because they love you," said Effie.

The princess whirled, planted both hands on her hips, and glared at the older woman. "Love isn't the issue, Effie. Freedom is. I'm a princess, yet I am less free than any peasant."

"Nonsense," said Effie sharply. "You are no peasant, my dear. And many's the person who would envy you the freedom you *do* have."

Briar Rose's eyes filled with tears. Effie's husband and sons were peasants who worked hard to make a living from the land. And Effie was right—they had far fewer freedoms—and luxuries—than she did.

"Oh, I'm sorry, Effie. I didn't mean to sound so petty and selfish. It's just that—"

Pulling Briar Rose to her, Effie murmured, "I know, lamb. I know. But you wait and see. Once you're past 16, things will be different."

"Are you sure?" mumbled Briar Rose, her voice muffled by Effie's sleeve.

"I'm sure. There are reasons why your parents keep you here in the kingdom, Briar Rose. Good reasons."

"So I've been told," sighed the princess. She pulled back and looked Effie in the eye, smiling slightly. "But no one ever explains exactly what those reasons are. No matter how often I ask, people just turn all funny and change the subject. So what is it, Effie? Are they afraid I'll be stolen by gypsies? Sold into slavery? Eaten by a dragon?"

"It's not for me to say, Your Majesty," replied Effie.

"Fine," said Briar Rose, her smile disappearing. "Then I'll not bother you anymore today." With that, she turned and practically ran down the hallway.

Effie stared after the fleeing figure and sighed loudly. Shaking her head, she said, "I'll be glad when this birthday has come and gone; when the princess is finally 16. Then I'll know she's safe. All of us who love her will finally be able to breathe easily."

Briar Rose didn't hear a word of this. She kept running until she reached her bedchamber, where she slammed the door with an angry thud. Throwing herself onto her four-poster bed, she peered up at the heavily embroidered canopy.

As so often happened once she thought about things, the princess felt guilty about her behavior. Once again, she had disappointed Effie—and her parents. Oh, she knew they all loved her, no matter how she acted. But she also knew that they wished she wouldn't question their decisions so often—or so loudly. They wished that she were just a bit more obedient and ladylike, as a proper princess should be.

But neither obedience nor ladylike behavior came easily to Briar Rose. They never had. Not that she was bad or ill-mannered. She always tried to be kind to others, even cranky old Malcolm, who swept the courtyards. She did her embroidery as neatly as possible, though her stitches were never quite right. She attended to her lessons, even on sunny days when she hated being trapped inside with dusty manuscripts. And she prided herself on her honesty and on the fact that she never broke a promise. Though she had to admit that she had bent one or two on occasion.

At last the princess lost interest in the bed canopy and got up. She walked over to one of the tall, narrow windows set into her chamber wall. There she leaned her forehead against the cold stones and peered out.

Below her, the courtyard was its usual bustle of activity. Carts of turnips, straw, and firewood were being trundled to the castle storerooms. A dark-haired boy rolled a barrel of cider toward the kitchen door. Near the stables, grooms ran back and forth and shouted to one another as they cared for their knight's horses. Several page boys stood around the well, laughing and talking among themselves.

And she was here in her bedchamber—alone, cranky,

and feeling sorry for herself. At that thought, the princess had to laugh.

"It seems that the only one I'm punishing is myself," she admitted aloud. "Just because I can't go hunting, I don't have to stay here. Not on such a glorious day."

Feeling more lighthearted, Briar Rose left the room and headed down the long, curving stairway. Along the way, she looked for Effie, intending to apologize. However, she reached the entry hall without seeing her.

Briar Rose made her way into the sunny courtyard, her soft slippers almost silent on the stones. She walked toward the drawbridge, exchanging friendly greetings along the way. At the castle gate, the princess nodded to the guards who stood there. Then she stepped out onto the surface of the drawbridge and paused.

The wooden structure led across a dry moat filled with wildflowers. On the other side, a dusty road beckoned, curving gently in the distance. Just around the bend, Briar Rose knew, lay a small village and the vast green fields farmed by Effie's husband and many others.

"Soon," the princess whispered. "Soon I'll be out there again; and one day I shall even go beyond Cambria."

But for now, Briar Rose decided, she would have to find some other form of entertainment. Perhaps I can find a visiting minstrel and get him to teach me a new tune, she thought.

With that in mind, the princess turned. As she passed through the gate, her skirt caught on one of the two rose

bushes that grew just inside. She untangled the fabric, being careful of the sharp thorns.

Briar Rose smiled. Her father had planted the bushes in honor of her birth, she knew. And for 15 seasons, they had borne only leaves and thorns—never a blossom. The gardener complained bitterly, but the bushes stubbornly defeated his best efforts to make them flower.

My roses aren't obedient either, the princess thought. Not to the gardener. Not even to the laws of nature.

5

To the Tower

Two days later, Briar Rose was again pleading with her parents. "Stay in my chambers? All day? Why am I being punished? What awful thing have I done now?"

"This is not a punishment," said the queen. "It is merely a request. Your birthday celebration is coming up. We are simply asking that you stay in your chambers until then. It is only for one day, after all."

"Yes," retorted the princess. "And it's the day before my birthday. That's hardly a time when I should be imprisoned in my chambers. Why? That is all I am asking."

"There are reasons," murmured her mother.

"What reasons?" demanded Briar Rose. She barely resisted the urge to stamp her feet and pout.

Her father and mother looked at one another in silence. Then the king said, "Turning 16 is an important and special event, Briar Rose. There is much we want to do to prepare for a proper birthday celebration. It will be easier if you are not underfoot. So we are asking you to stay in the castle."

"In your bedchamber," the queen corrected her husband.

"But I won't get underfoot," protested the princess. "I'll stay out of the kitchen. I'll even stay out of the great hall, if that's what you want."

"We want your word that you will obey us in this matter, my dear," the king said firmly.

Briar Rose knew when she was defeated. Frowning, she said, "I promise to stay put."

Her parents looked relieved, though Briar Rose had not said *where* she would stay put. Failing to notice this fine point, King Walter smiled and said, "It's settled then. We will check in on you often tomorrow, dear."

That evening, as she prepared for bed, Briar Rose seethed. Her parents had always been overprotective. Everyone in Cambria had—even her brothers to some degree. But this was ridiculous. Now she was a prisoner in her own room. And to make things worse, on the day before her birthday!

The next day passed as slowly as Briar Rose had anticipated it would. Her father visited early in the morning and wished her well. Her mother stopped by so they could spend an hour together doing needlework. And Effie popped in and out several times.

Despite their company, the princess hated the feeling of being trapped inside. And even worse, she was bored.

She tried to read, but couldn't concentrate on the words. She attempted to work on her embroidery, but only ended up having to undo much of what she had already done. She stared out the window, but that merely made her think about what she was missing.

As the day dragged on, Briar Rose grew more and more restless. She knew the king and queen expected her to stay in her room. However, she also knew that she hadn't actually promised to do so. She clearly remembered only promising to "stay put." And, she reasoned, that didn't necessarily mean staying put in the same spot all day. Besides, what harm could it do to leave for a short time? She would keep away from the most public areas. Then she couldn't be accused of getting underfoot and disturbing the birthday preparations.

After all, Briar Rose told herself, she really *should* stretch her legs. It wasn't healthy for a growing girl to spend long hours being idle. Hadn't Effie told her that more than once? Her nurse had little patience with daydreaming about adventure and excitement.

So, an hour before the evening meal was scheduled to arrive, Briar Rose decided to make her escape. She could be back before her absence was discovered, she was sure. With this plan in mind, the princess slowly opened her chamber door. She noted with satisfaction the emptiness of the hall, then slipped outside.

Briar Rose headed for the staircase at the end of the long hallway. But instead of going down, she went up, toward the western corner of the castle. She had always loved visiting the high tower that stood there. It hadn't been used in years, so Briar Rose felt that the tower was her secret hideaway. Surely it would do no harm to spend an hour or so there, gazing out over the fields and woods.

The stairs gradually narrowed and began to spiral upward. After ten minutes of climbing, Briar Rose reached the top. She paused to catch her breath, then pushed the heavy wooden door open.

To her amazement, someone was already there!

6

A Curse Fulfilled

A woman stood in the center of the room, a basket of gray sheep's wool at her feet. Beside her, a large wheel whirled merrily on its wooden stand. The woman was thin and bony, with long, tangled black hair and pointed fingernails.

"Wh-wh-who are you?" stammered Briar Rose. "And what are you doing here?"

At the princess' words, the woman looked toward the door. "Ah, Princess, how good to see you again," she said in a raspy voice.

"Pardon me, madam, but should I know you?" asked Briar Rose.

"You should, my dear, but you obviously don't. I am Cassandra," the woman said. Then she waited, watching the princess closely.

Briar Rose shook her head. "I am sorry, but I don't recognize your name."

"I am not surprised, I suppose," said the woman. "Few people in your kingdom seem to remember me."

"Forgive me for seeming rude," Briar Rose said. "It's just that I don't understand what you are doing here. This tower is never used and no one except me ever seems to even visit it."

"Be that as it may, I am here," said Cassandra. "Are you going to banish me from your tower?"

"Of course not," replied Briar Rose. "I was just curious, that's all."

"Ah, yes," said the woman. "Your curiosity is most understandable, my child." Then she bent her head and went back to work, ignoring her visitor.

Briar Rose moved closer to see what was going on. With one hand, the woman turned the great wheel. With the other, she held a twisted rope of wool. It wound around the twirling wheel, magically becoming a rough thread as it did so. The thread wrapped itself around a device at the far end of the wooden stand that supported the wheel.

"What are you doing?" asked Briar Rose.

"Why, I am spinning thread to make cloth," said Cassandra. "Surely you're seen it done before."

"Never," admitted the princess. "I have seen thread, of course. The royal weaver uses it to make his beautiful cloth. But his thread comes from lands far away, just as Cook's spices do."

"Ah," said Cassandra. "I see. Well, you are most welcome to watch me work, Your Highness. If you are interested in such a simple task, of course."

"Oh, I am," said Briar Rose. She pulled a small stool closer to the spinning wheel. For a few moments she looked on in fascination, almost hypnotized by the motion.

Then Cassandra's voice broke the silence. "Spinning is not all that difficult, you know. Would you like to try it yourself?"

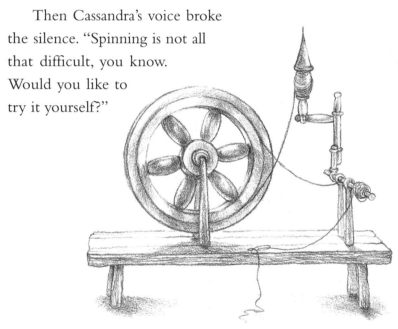

"I would. Very much so," said Briar Rose. "That is, if you don't mind showing me how."

"Mind? Of course I don't mind," said Cassandra. "After all, you are the princess, and I am merely a loyal subject, happy to do your bidding." She motioned Briar Rose to come closer. "Here, stand at the end of the wheel."

In her excitement, Briar Rose didn't note the measured look Cassandra gave her. She eagerly followed the woman's bidding. "Now, what do I do?" she asked.

"First, you need to check the spindle," said Cassandra. She pointed to the device on which the thread had been wound. "Just pick it up in your right hand."

As Briar Rose took the spindle, she felt a prick. "Oh, it's sharp!" she cried. She looked down at a single drop of blood that oozed from her thumb.

To her surprise, Cassandra didn't seem at all concerned. Instead, she began to laugh. It was an evil sound that echoed from the tower walls, then cut off abruptly as the woman vanished.

However, Briar Rose hadn't heard a thing beyond that first terrible burst of laughter. Immediately afterward, she had slumped from the stool to the floor. Now she lay there, looking as if she were dead.

7
Aftermath

At the moment Briar Rose fell asleep, so did every other living thing in the castle and its courtyard. Cook, who had been stirring a pot of porridge, dozed beside the dying fire. A serving maid in the great hall fell asleep with her cleaning cloth in hand. Nearby, Effie snored softly on a bench.

The king and queen had been talking in the throne room. Their conversation ended mid-sentence and both went into a deep and dreamless sleep, their hands almost touching.

In the courtyard, page boys now slept with only the stony ground as their pillows. Pigeons had ceased their endless cooing. They roosted peacefully on the stable rooftop, their heads tucked under their wings. The horses slept standing up in their stables. Even the flies on the walls were sound asleep.

At the castle gate, the guards had dropped their swords and slumped against the wall. So they hadn't noticed when the drawbridge mysteriously rose, sealing the castle off from the rest of the kingdom.

Then the rose bushes just inside the gate began to grow—and grow—and grow. Thick, thorny branches twined up and over the castle walls. There they continued to creep from stone to stone. In a matter of hours, nothing could be seen except a mass of branches and thorns. It loomed silently over the sunlit clearing.

The villagers in their homes and shops and the peasants in the distant fields were hard at work. They had no inkling of what had happened to their castle. Not until later, when several peasants approached, their carts loaded with the day's harvest.

Word spread quickly. The castle was gone—hidden in a fortress of thorns. And, apparently, those inside were gone as well. Uneasiness filled every heart—and sorrow as well. Especially on the part of those whose loved ones had been working in the castle.

Soon afterward, Hugh and William neared the end of their homeward journey. As they rode into the village, several men ran toward them.

"Your Highnesses!" one man shouted. "Wait!"

The young princes pulled their horses to a stop. Between gasping breaths, the man managed to say, "The castle, Your Majesties! The castle!"

"What are you talking about, my good fellow?" asked Hugh, a bit impatiently. "We are headed there now."

"But it's gone, sire!"

"Gone?" repeated William. "Whatever do you mean?"

"It is hidden behind a wall of thorns, Your Majesty," another man responded. "That's what he means."

The brothers looked at each other in horror. "Cassandra's curse!" cried William. "Can this be it?"

"Impossible!" responded Hugh. "Briar Rose is safe in Cambria where there are no spindles. And she will be 16 tomorrow. There is no way this could have happened. Not now!"

The two princes galloped off down the road. As they rounded the curve leading to the castle, an awful sight greeted them. They had hoped to see a lowered drawbridge and the reflection of the setting sun on stone walls. Instead they saw only a solid mass of thorny branches. The scene was exactly as the villagers had described it.

A small band of men and women stood nearby, some weeping. William spotted Effie's husband at the center of the group and went to him at once.

"What can we do?" asked the old man as the prince leapt off his horse. "We have tried to cut through the branches, but our scythes and hoes only break."

By now Hugh had joined William. Without a word, the princes drew their swords and advanced on the thorny barricade.

However, they had no better luck than the farmers. Their swords merely clanged against the thick, woody wall, doing no damage whatsoever.

After several more attempts, darkness forced the princes to give up. Heartsick, they returned to the village for the night. No one slept, wondering what the morning would bring.

The next day, the first thing Hugh and William did was to summon Miranda. "Is there anything you can do?" Hugh asked when the Wise Woman arrived.

"I am sorry, but the answer is no," said Miranda softly. "I had feared that Cassandra would find a way to make good her curse, and she did. But remember that your sister is not dead, my lords. She is merely asleep."

"She may as well be dead," said William bitterly. "And our parents with her. For we shall never see them again in our lifetimes."

"You are right about that, I am afraid," Miranda replied. "Cassandra was furious when she realized that the princess and the others are merely asleep. She has sworn that no one will be allowed to rescue Briar Rose. But she cannot undo that part of my gift, my lords. So I can promise you this: in 100 years, a brave man will come forth. If he can best Cassandra, he will save Briar Rose and those trapped with her. Until then, there is nothing anyone can do."

With those words echoing in their minds, Hugh and William retired to another of Cambria's castles. They spent months consulting with the bravest and wisest knights of the kingdom, unwilling to accept Miranda's declaration that nothing could be done. Many of these men tried to defeat the wall of thorns, but none were successful.

And then, one young knight who had gone out to attack the wall disappeared. "This is Cassandra's work," said Hugh when he heard the news. "She vowed that no one would get to Briar Rose. Now she is keeping that promise by destroying any who try."

Sadly, the brothers issued a proclamation. No one else was to risk his life attempting to get through the thorns. Still, some did, only to die trying. Or so it was supposed, as they were never seen again. The only evidence of their attempts was the occasional abandoned sword found lying at the base of the thorny wall.

As the years passed, a forest slowly grew up around what had been Briar Rose's castle. William and Hugh and the others who had lost loved ones lived out their lives and died, still mourning.

Within two generations, few spoke of the castle or of those locked in sleep behind its walls. And even fewer tried in vain to rescue the princess.

Briar Rose and her companions were all but forgotten.

Book 2

The Prince

𝟖

Galen's Quest

Prince Galen removed his plumed hat and scratched his head. His dark eyes studied the crossroads ahead.

"Where shall we go now, Micah?" he asked. Then he frowned. "Already I'm reduced to talking to my horse. This is not exactly the exciting life of adventure I had imagined."

Galen thought about the past six weeks. He had upset his father, King Frederick of Avondale, when he had announced that he was leaving to seek adventure.

"Your place is here," his father had objected, "with your brother and me."

"My brother will be Avondale's next king, Father, not I," said Galen. "Though I hope for a long and healthy life for you before that day comes," he added quickly. "I am only the younger son, and must seek my own fortune."

The king could hardly argue this point with Galen. The kingdom would pass to his eldest son, Galen's brother. That was how it had always been in Avondale.

"It's not that I resent being the younger son," Galen explained further. "It's more that I want to do something,

Father. To find out exactly who I am and what I want to accomplish with my life. To seek a quest. To have an adventure!"

"Adventure?" his father had protested. "You can find plenty of adventure right here."

But Galen hadn't agreed with that. His head was filled with stories of bold knights and fearsome dragons. With tournaments and battles and lovely maidens whose hearts waited to be won by handsome young princes. None of that, he was sure, could be found in peaceful Avondale.

At last the king had bowed to Galen's wishes and given his blessing. "Find adventure, then, my boy," he had said. "But don't entirely forget us. We shall be awaiting your return."

Galen assured his father that he would be back in due time. Then he outfitted his horse and left as soon as he decently could.

Now, after weeks on the road, the prince was weary. Oh, he had had many new experiences, to be sure. But none of them could be considered even slightly adventurous. He had single-handedly fixed a broken wheel on an elderly peasant's cart. But that was hardly a save-the-world kind of deed. At a village fair, he had seen performers who ate fire. But he hadn't seen any evidence of a fierce, fire-breathing dragon just waiting to be conquered. He had visited tournament after tournament. But since he was not a proper knight, he could only dream of being a champion. And he had encountered princesses galore. But all of them, in his opinion, were silly and spoiled.

Galen sighed and put his mind to choosing his next destination. The road ahead branched off in several directions. The top of the signpost pointed east and bore the legend "Milltown." That didn't interest Galen. He had seen all he wanted to of small towns, which he felt to be sadly lacking in adventure.

The prince studied the other destinations laid out before him. A city would be interesting, he thought. And there was a sign pointing the way to a large one—off to the northwest. "We are sure to find some excitement in such a place, Micah," Galen said. He pulled on the reins to guide his horse in that direction.

For hours, they rode along the dusty road. To Galen's surprise, he encountered few travelers going the same way. Once he passed a caravan of gypsies headed in the opposite direction. However, for the most part, the road stretched out ahead, empty and silent.

By late afternoon, Galen realized that the city would not be reached that day. He began to contemplate sleeping in the open rather than in the comfort of a cozy inn. "I suppose that will be something of an adventure," he said. "Though there is nothing especially brave or noble about a rocky bed."

Then the prince crested a hill and saw a small castle standing guard across the valley. The road wound its way downhill, along the shore of a narrow lake, and up to the castle. Fading sunlight danced on the water and cast long shadows on the hillside.

Though he hated to admit it, Galen was relieved at the sight. The prince clucked to his horse and headed for this welcome sanctuary. In less than an hour, he was riding past well-tended fields toward the castle gate.

"What ho, visitor?" a guard called.

"I am Prince Galen of Avondale," Galen announced. "And I seek a night's lodging."

"You are welcome, then, my lord," said the guard. He stood back and Galen rode into a bustling courtyard.

A young groom came at once to take Micah. Galen dismounted and tossed him a gold coin. The boy caught the coin in one hand, then bit it to test its quality. "Thank you kindly, sir!" he said with a grin. "I'll see that your animal is watered and fed."

Galen made his way into the castle itself. As was usually the case, he wasn't the only visitor. The great hall was half full of people, some still bearing the dust of the road. Before long, the tired traveler was seated, enjoying a hearty meal.

After eating, Galen sat contentedly, watching and listening. Close by, an old knight was entertaining several squires with tales of past tournaments. Across the table, a lord and lady flirted madly, ignoring everyone around them. Near the door of the great hall, a colorfully dressed juggler demonstrated his skills. And off to one side, a troubadour strummed his lute and began to sing.

At first Galen paid no attention to the troubadour's song. His stomach was full and he was weary from the day's travels. So he sat on the bench, almost dozing.

But then he caught a line—something about a princess needing rescue in a kingdom far away. He got up and moved closer, the better to hear the troubadour. He arrived just as the song wound to its end.

Seeing Galen approach, the troubadour smiled. "Ah, a fine gentleman to hear my feeble voice," he said. "Shall I sing something for you, my lord?"

"Yes," said Galen. "The same song you just finished, if you would."

Nodding, the troubadour strummed a few notes, then began to sing. Galen listened intently to the words:

High in a tower, a princess sleeps.
Lost in time, her life has ceased.
Beauty undimmed, she lies forlorn
Trapped within a prison of thorn;
Trapped 'til a man brave and true
Rends the thorns for her rescue;
Climbs stony steps to see her face
And with a kiss shares his grace.
He who saves her, stalwart man,
Will win her heart, and her hand.
'Tis no task for those weak of will;
Though many have tried, and do so still.
Princes and knights have met their fates
And died there at the castle gate.

The troubadour's song struck a chord in Galen. An imprisoned princess! A danger-filled rescue! Even if there was no dragon involved, this seemed to be an adventure worthy of his attention.

As the last notes faded in the air, Galen handed the troubadour a coin. Then he asked, "Tell me, good fellow, what is the kingdom where this maiden is to be found?"

"They say she is a princess of Cambria, my lord."

"Cambria!" said Galen in surprise. "I have never heard of such a place. Is there any truth to your song?"

The troubadour shrugged. "'Tis only a song my grandfather sang, sir. And his grandfather before him. To be honest, I do not know if it is true or not."

"I see," said Galen. He tossed another coin to the troubadour, then returned to his bench. His thoughts were of the song he had just heard—and of the adventure it promised.

Long after he had bedded down on a straw mat on the floor, Galen tossed restlessly. His dreams were a jumble of towers and thorns, fallen knights, and forbidding gates. And a lovely princess in need of rescue.

He woke exhausted—and determined to find out if the tale was true.

An Old Man's Tale

Galen sighed and settled back on the hard bench. He was sitting in a dark corner of a dark and dreary inn. Everywhere he had traveled for the past two days, he had asked questions about Cambria. He had heard some whispers of its existence but nothing definite. In fact, few seemed to even recognize the name. Until now.

When the prince had first entered the inn, he had asked about Cambria. Most of the occupants had shrugged and returned to their conversations. All but an old man in the far corner. In a trembling voice, he had said, "Cambria. Aye, my lord, I've heard of the place."

So Galen had sat down next to the ancient fellow. "My name is Edgar," the man had confided. Then he had gone on to say, "Why, I have even been to Cambria myself. For a tournament many years ago. I was a groom for Sir Francis of Woodstock, you see."

Galen's interest had set Edgar off on a long story about when Sir Francis faced the champion of Dragonswood. And after that, another story, equally long.

Though Galen had many questions for Edgar, he knew they would have to wait. At least until this tale was told.

At last, Edgar paused for a swallow of cider. Before he could begin another story, Galen asked, "So, good man, what have you heard about the princess?"

"Princess?" echoed Edgar vaguely. "What princess would that be, sire?"

"The princess of Cambria," Galen reminded the old gentleman. "The one who is said to be missing."

"Ah, yes, *that* princess. Well, to be sure, I have actually heard more about a missing king and queen," admitted Edgar. "'Tis said they vanished many long years ago. Along with an entire castle and their daughter. That would be your princess, I wager."

"Do you know anything more? What happened to make them disappear? And where in Cambria can this castle be found?"

"I don't know any of that," answered Edgar. "All I know is that some say the castle's disappearance is why Cambria's fortunes faded over the years. Others say there is a curse on the place. Of course, I got that from a Cambrian knight who performed sadly in a tournament. He could have been making excuses for his lack of skill on the jousting field. Unlike Sir Francis, who—"

Galen allowed his mind to wander. He had heard all he wanted to about Sir Francis's exploits. He wasn't interested in long-ago tournaments, fading fortunes, or curses. He was only interested in getting to Cambria—and finding the sort of adventure that seemed to wait there for anyone brave enough to seek it. Surely if anyone could save the princess, he could. That is, if she actually did exist.

Something told him she did.

She *had* to.

Saving her was now his quest.

10

Cambria

Galen had been within the borders of Cambria for half a day. Still, he had learned nothing more of a princess trapped in a thorny prison.

It had been a long and difficult trip to get this far. The mountains that formed Cambria's eastern border had almost defeated the prince. Even sure-footed Micah had stumbled on the narrow and rocky paths. High in the deserted mountain range, the nights had been cold and frighteningly lonely. Yet Galen had never given up. Something drove him onward, forcing him to move as quickly as possible. He had an even greater sense of urgency now—a feeling that something important waited for him.

The prince rode through a dense forest of oak and pine. While still hilly, the land had flattened out enough that he occasionally came across a fellow traveler. However, most of them looked upon him with more than a little suspicion. When he asked about a princess, some acted as if he had taken leave of his senses. At best, they listened politely to his query, then shook their heads. It seemed that no one shared old Edgar's belief that such a princess actually existed.

"Cambria has no princesses, my lord," he heard more than once. "Imprisoned or otherwise."

And one gentleman's response to Galen's question was even stranger. "Princess?" he had said. "There are no princesses to be found here, my lord. For that matter, Cambria has no king or queen, either. Merely a regent, managing the kingdom. And doing a poor job of that, I might add."

Galen had no time to waste on matters such as the management of the kingdom. So he merely nodded and went on his way. He preferred to think of the challenges ahead. A wall of thorns didn't sound all that difficult to handle. A few whacks with his sword should take care of it, he thought. There was sure to be something more exciting waiting once that was done. A dark knight or a fierce dragon who guarded the princess, perhaps. Some sort of challenge worthy of a prince on a great quest.

"No matter what foes I must face," Galen told Micah, "I will save this princess. I feel it in my bones."

The horse nickered softly, which encouraged the prince slightly. So did the fact that the forest was beginning to thin out. At last the trees were far enough apart that the warm June sunshine could trickle through their branches and dapple the road with its brightness.

Micah's hooves echoed dully and kicked up puffs of dust. Lulled by the motion, and suffering from sleeping on the ground for several nights, Galen almost dozed off.

Suddenly Micah snorted and danced sideways, nearly unseating his rider. "Whoa!" cried Galen, grabbing hold of the reins.

He saw at once what had spooked the horse. A bundle of gray rags lay at the side of the road. And it was moving! It was a human being, Galen realized with horror. An old woman who lay in a heap, moaning softly.

Galen was tempted to keep riding. He wanted nothing to interfere with his search for the mysterious princess. However, his kind heart wouldn't allow him to ignore someone in need.

In a moment, he was off his horse and on his knees in the dust.

"What is the matter, mistress?" he asked. "Are you injured?"

The woman moaned again through parched lips. Galen slipped

his waterskin off his shoulder and gently raised the woman's head. Holding the vessel to her lips, he said softly, "Drink. Just a little now, until you have recovered."

The woman took a few sips, then let her head fall back onto Galen's arm. "Thank you kindly, sir," she said in a feathery whisper. Then she fell into a faint.

Galen stared down at her with pity. He couldn't leave her here by the roadside. She would surely die of thirst and hunger. There was only one thing to do. He had to take her with him.

Slowly Galen gathered the woman into his arms and stood up. She weighed almost nothing, he noted. He sat the woman atop Micah's back, where she promptly slumped forward onto the animal's neck. Then, holding

the woman in place with one hand, Galen led his horse down the road.

They hadn't gone far when the woman opened her faded blue eyes. She struggled to sit up. "No!" she cried weakly.

"I mean you no harm, good woman," said Galen, bringing Micah to a halt. "Do not be afraid."

"I am not afraid," responded the woman in a faint voice. "But my home lies to the east. In the mountains. Won't you please take me there?"

Galen looked into the old woman's strained face. East was hardly the direction he wanted to go. Not when he felt that every step westward was moving him closer to his goal. Still, he couldn't leave the woman here where she would surely die.

Finally he nodded and said, "I will take you where you want." Then, his heart heavy, he turned the horse around and headed back the way he had come.

They journeyed together for the rest of the day. As the hours passed, the woman regained enough strength to sit erect on Micah's back. Soon she began to talk. She told Galen that she had been set upon by robbers. They had chased her horse off and left her for dead.

Then she began to ask questions of her rescuer. "What is your name, my lord? And where are you headed?"

To his surprise, Galen found himself unburdening his

soul to the old woman. He told her his name and shared his desire for adventure. He described his quest and how hopeless it seemed, even now that he was in Cambria.

"A princess, you say?" murmured the woman. "Trapped in a thorny prison? And needing rescue?"

"That is what the troubadour sang of," sighed Galen. "And that is what my heart tells me is true. No matter how many people say the princess does not exist."

"Follow your heart, my lord," said the old woman softly. Then she fell silent. In fact, it was almost dark before she spoke next.

"Here!" the woman cried out. Startled, Galen jerked his horse to a halt.

"This is my home," she continued. "You can leave me now and get on with your quest."

Galen looked around in confusion. There was no shelter in sight. Just a towering oak tree.

"But I can't abandon you in the forest, good woman," he said. "Where is your home? I see no sign of it here."

"I told you, Prince Galen, *this* is my home," she said. "This forest." Her voice sounded different somehow. "Now if you would help me down."

When Galen turned to lift her from the horse, he stared in amazement. This was no old woman before him. It was a beautiful young one, with dark brown eyes and golden curls that glowed strangely in the fading light.

"What . . . ? Who . . . ? I mean . . ."

"My name is Miranda," said the woman. "And as I told you, this is my home, Galen. You see, I am one of the Wise Women of the forest."

Galen gazed at her in awe. Since reaching Cambria, he had heard tales of the Wise Women, but had thought them merely legends.

"But why were you lying there by the road?" he asked when he could finally speak. "In the form of an old woman and looking as if you were dead?"

"I needed to judge the goodness of your heart," Miranda said. "Now I know that you are worthy of my princess."

"Your princess?" he cried, looking at her with shining eyes. "Then she *does* exist?"

"Yes," said Miranda softly. "The time has come to rescue her, Galen. But it will not be easy. You will have to use your wits. And it will be dangerous."

"I don't care about that," declared Galen. His mind suddenly filled with an image of himself charging forward on Micah, ready to do battle. A brave knight to the rescue, *that* was his destiny. And no challenge, no matter how frightening, could stop him.

"I have a quest!" he cried. "I will save her—even if it costs me my life."

As these brave words left his mouth, a cloud blotted out the late-day sun. Galen shivered in the sudden chill.

11

Miranda's Charm

"**Y**ou must listen carefully to my words," Miranda said. The two of them had settled under the great oak tree to talk.

She went on to tell Galen of the curse Cassandra had put on the beautiful princess of Cambria. And of her own attempt to soften it by causing the princess to sleep instead.

"The 100 years have come to an end at last," said Miranda in conclusion. "And I have been waiting for the one who will save Briar Rose."

"So all I have to do is find the princess and kiss her, and she will wake?" asked Galen. He tried to keep the disappointment out of his voice. This task hardly seemed difficult—or dangerous.

"Yes," replied Miranda. "But it won't be as easy as it sounds. For one thing, I am not the only one who has been waiting to see how this story unravels. Cassandra has spent the last century plotting ways to get past my charm. She will do everything within her considerable power to keep the princess trapped in her prison of sleep."

"Can she do it?" asked Galen. "Can she keep Briar Rose from waking?"

"Yes—if she can stop *you*."

For a long time Galen was quiet, thinking about what lay ahead of him. He had to find the castle, long hidden behind a vast wall of thorns. Then make his way safely through the clutching branches, find Briar Rose, and kiss her. All the while avoiding the evil Cassandra. Perhaps this was an exciting task after all.

"I can do it," he said at last. "I *will* do it!"

"I thought you would say that," said Miranda. "I cannot come with you, Galen, but I can point you in the right direction. You will find the castle due west of this spot—a journey of less than two days. You must keep a sharp eye out to find it, as it is well hidden. And now, before you go, I have a small gift for you."

Miranda held out her hand, in which a small velvet bag had mysteriously appeared. "Wear the medallion inside around your neck. It will offer you some assistance if you use it wisely. And it will provide you with a weapon against Cassandra."

Galen loosened the drawstrings of the bag and emptied the contents into the palm of his hand. A simple heart-shaped medallion sparkled there, suspended from a fine chain of gold. A crooked line was etched across the heart's surface, from top to bottom. The only other ornamentation consisted of tiny letters engraved along the outside edges of the heart.

Galen read the inscription aloud, " 'To save a heart, break a heart.' Is this a riddle? What do the words mean?"

"You will have to figure that out for yourself, I'm afraid," replied Miranda. "I can offer you no further help in the matter. However, I can give you a warning to share with Briar Rose once she has been awakened. Tell her to beware. Cassandra will be angry at having her curse foiled. She may seek revenge."

"What can she—what can *we*—do about that?"

To his surprise, there was no response from the Wise Woman. When Galen looked up, he was alone. Miranda had vanished.

12

A Wall of Thorns

Two days later, Galen sat astride his horse, staring at yet another crossroads. Despite Miranda's assurances that Briar Rose did exist, doubts were beginning to fill him. He had spoken to everyone he met as he journeyed deeper into Cambria. No one would admit to believing in the princess, though some had heard of her.

"Aye, my lord," one gray-haired peasant had said as he leaned on his hoe. "I remember my granny telling that story. An old wives' tale, she called it."

"A princess trapped by thorns?" said a young duke when their paths crossed. "I, too, have heard the story, but hardly find it believable. I think someone is jesting, sir."

Now Galen wasn't sure what to do. He had been heading due west, just as Miranda had told him to do. But the crossroads he had just reached offered no way west as an option. A wide, hard-packed road led off to the north. Another, smaller and dustier, headed southeast. And a third, little more than a hunting trail, struck off to the south.

As Galen stared at the choices before him, he absentmindedly rubbed the heart medallion that now hung around his neck.

Then he blinked. What was that? The light had shifted slightly, as if something had passed over the sun. But a quick glance at the summer sky showed it to be clear and cloudless. Still, whether it was a trick of the light or not, he had seen *something* odd straight ahead.

He slid off Micah's back and walked forward a few paces. Then he bent down to study the ground more closely. There was a faint depression in the earth. It was almost completely hidden by the tall grasses and wildflowers that grew in profusion.

Galen traced the depression with his fingers. An old wagon rut, he was sure. As if people had once traveled this way, but not for many, many years.

His decision made, Galen got back on his horse. He rode straight ahead, into the meadow. The grasses tickled Micah's belly and slapped against Galen's feet. Lemony sunshine lit the fields and danced on the flowers and leaves. Except, Galen noted, for an occasional shadowy spot where a thick, grayish fog seemed to hug the ground. Strange, he thought, on such a pleasant day. Then he dismissed the fog from his mind.

Using the sun as his compass, Galen forged ahead all that afternoon. The air was warm and filled with darting dragonflies. Several times his passing flushed a rabbit or pheasant from the underbrush. But other than the wild things of the meadow, there was no sign of life.

Gradually the fields gave way to woods, then to a proper forest. Still Galen continued west. He veered from his course only to avoid outcroppings of rock or the widest parts of the many streams he had to cross.

Then, as he made his way around a particularly large rock, he saw something blocking his path.

Galen slid off Micah's back and tied the reins to a branch. Sword in hand, he advanced toward the obstacle ahead.

It was a wall of branches. They twisted and turned, weaving a solid blanket that completely hid what lay behind. Every branch was covered with thick thorns, each longer than a man's finger.

Heart beating wildly, Galen paced off the wall. It was at least 100 feet long. When he rounded the corner, he saw that the wall continued for an even greater distance. By his estimate, it had to be 40 feet high—and there was no telling its thickness.

Excitement coursed through the young prince. He had found Cambria's missing castle at last—and the princess he sought had to be hidden inside!

13

The Broken Heart

Galen dashed back to the center of the wall. Raising his sword high overhead, he swung it down in a fierce blow.

It was if he had struck a wall of iron. There was an earsplitting clang. His arm quivered as the sword reflected the force of the blow.

Again Galen slashed at the thorny branches. This time the sword sprang back at him angrily, causing him to drop it.

The prince stepped back to study the wall. There had to be a way in. He reached out and grabbed hold of one branch, trying to avoid the thorns. Then he pulled.

The wall seemed to come alive! One branch twisted around the prince's arm, grasping his sleeve in a thorny grip. Then slowly, the wall began to quiver, pulling Galen toward its center as if he were caught in quicksand.

A wild laugh filled the forest, echoing off trees and branches. Desperately, Galen tried to free his arm—and to find the source of the awful sound.

"So you think you can save the princess, do you?"

Galen turned his head in the direction of the voice. A cloud of dark, gray mist swirled in the air, creating a whirlwind of leaves. Then a tall, thin woman robed in black gradually materialized from the mist. At her appearance, Micah reared up in fear. The reins snapped and the horse ran off, his hooves clattering on the stony ground.

Cassandra—for Galen knew it must be she—now extended one arm. The thorny wall began to move faster, as if it were boiling just below the surface. To his horror, Galen felt himself being sucked further into the branches.

"You fool!" cried Cassandra. "You will join the others who have tried to save her. Your bones shall be added to theirs! Did you think I would allow her to be rescued? Never! Not when her parents refused to treat me with the same respect they showed to my miserable sisters."

Then, with one last horrible laugh, she disappeared. Nothing remained of her except the gray mist. In a few moments, that too vanished.

Though Galen continued to struggle frantically, the hold of the thorns only tightened. His arm was becoming numb and his strength was fading. Was this how it was to end, then? Was he to die here, without ever seeing the princess?

It can't be, he thought. It was one thing to die in battle while a lovely princess looked on and admired his bravery. It was entirely another to be beaten by a bush, no matter how thorny.

And worse still, Miranda had hinted that this might be the last chance to rescue the princess.

"No!" gasped Galen, renewing his struggles. "I won't give up! I won't let Cassandra and her evil win!" He thought the grip of the thorns lessened at his words. However, it wasn't enough to allow him to pull his arm free.

Suddenly the prince remembered the medallion. Miranda had said it would help him. And surely he needed help now.

With his free hand, Galen grasped the medallion where it lay against his chest. "To save a heart, break a heart," he recited from memory. "I know the heart I am to save belongs to the princess. So perhaps *this* is the heart I need to break." He pushed down, snapping the medallion in two along the etched line.

For one horrible moment, he felt the broken piece begin to slip from his weary fingers. Just in time, he grasped it more securely. Then, using the jagged edge as a knife, he slashed fiercely at the thorns.

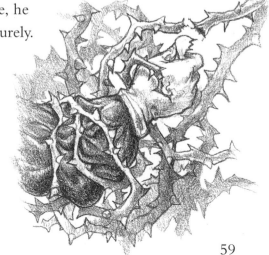

14

A Kiss

As the edge of the heart touched them, the thorns parted, freeing Galen from their grasp. Then they began to shrivel and shrink upward. In a matter of minutes, they disappeared over the top of a great stone wall. Set into it was a wooden drawbridge, raised to shut out intruders.

Galen stood there, breathing hard and wondering what to do next. He had found the castle. He had broken the grip of the thorns. But he could hardly rescue the princess if he couldn't get inside where she lay sleeping.

The prince paced back and forth, thinking. At last an idea came to him. It was hardly adventurous, but it should do the trick.

With his sword, Galen quickly cut branch after branch from nearby trees. These he laid out on the ground in a grid pattern. Then he fastened the branches together with smaller, more flexible ones. In two hours, he had created a rough ladder.

The prince carefully lifted the ladder and leaned it against the stone wall. It was too short, but it would have to do. He placed one foot on the first rung. Then, holding his breath, he lifted the other foot.

The rung bent, but held. Galen climbed slowly, one rung at a time. Once, his foot slipped and he almost tumbled back to the ground. But he managed to grab hold of a protruding stone.

At last he reached the top of the ladder. There was still 10 feet of wall to go. Gripping the stone surface as best he could, Galen pulled himself upward. His feet struggled to find a hold. Slowly he inched his way toward the top, depending on the roughness of the wall to offer him something to grasp.

Breathing heavily, Galen slipped over the edge. He fell onto a high walkway that stretched the length of the stone walls. A guard slept there, his sword at his side.

Barely glancing at the sleeping man, Galen hurried down the closest staircase and into the courtyard below. He was inside!

On each side of the closed drawbridge, guards leaned against the castle walls, their swords lying at their feet. Galen stepped around one guard and kept moving.

As the prince made his way across the courtyard, he noted an eerie silence. There were no sounds other than his own footsteps echoing on the stones. No insects buzzed, no birds twittered, no horses neighed. The quiet weighed down upon him.

Everywhere he looked, people and animals slept.

Some, like the guards, leaned against the nearest surface. Others had sunk to the ground and now lay there. Even the flies on the horses and the pigeons on the rooftops were still. It was as if every living thing had been captured and frozen in time.

"Hello!" cried Galen, desperate to break the silence. The echo of his voice was the only answer. The prince made a slow circle, looking in all directions. However, there was no sign of life to be seen—other than the sleepers. And none of them showed any response to his greeting.

Galen tried to shake off his sense of unease. Surely this was too simple. He half expected something—or someone—to jump out at him. And what about Cassandra? Would she allow him to find the princess and wake her? It hardly seemed likely.

His eyes traveled upward, studying the circular structures that stood at each corner of the castle. "The westernmost tower," he said to himself. "That's where Miranda said the princess sleeps." Cautiously, he made his way up a set of steps that led to a wide central door. As he climbed, he stepped around a boy, two dogs, and an archer—all asleep.

Once inside the castle proper, Galen stopped to get his bearings. The logs in the enormous fireplace had long ago dwindled to ashes. Still, the castle hardly looked as if it had been standing untended for a century. Goblets of shiny gold sat on a table, and tapestries still gleamed with rich colors. A young serving girl leaned against the wall, a cleaning rag clutched in her hand. Two dogs dozed underneath the table. And nearby, an older woman slept undisturbed on a wide bench.

Remembering Miranda's words, Galen searched for a stairway. As he passed a huge door, he glanced inside. A man and woman sat side by side on a pair of richly carved thrones. The king and queen—their crowns told him who they were—slept peacefully, their hands almost touching.

Galen kept on, opening doors and spying more sleeping people. Finally he found what he had been seeking—a staircase that spiraled steeply upward.

Drawing his sword, Galen started climbing. He went further and further, passing no one either asleep or awake. The stairway narrowed and the stone walls gradually closed in. The air seemed to become thicker and colder, wrapping itself around him like an icy cloak.

Several times Galen stopped and whirled to check the stairway behind him. Despite the feeling that someone was there, he saw nothing.

Then he realized that the air really *had* thickened. A dark mist wrapped around his feet and slowly began to form a cloud.

Cassandra! She was here!

Galen slashed at the cloud. As his sword entered it, ice formed on the blade. An evil laugh resounded off the walls.

"So near, my brave prince. So very near."

Galen could hear the words, but he couldn't see Cassandra. He realized that he had to do something before she materialized. And he realized that his sword was of little use against her.

The only thing that seemed to have any power to stop her was Miranda's medallion. Galen quickly reached for the half of the heart still around his neck and snatched it off, chain and all. Holding it, he plunged his hand into the cloud.

A cold unlike anything he had ever felt before came over him. Then there was a howl of rage—and the cloud dissolved.

Breathing heavily, Galen raced up the remaining steps toward a huge wooden door. Without hesitating, he pulled it open. The door protested, the creak of long-unused hinges echoing down the twisting stairwell.

Galen stepped over the threshold. There, lying on a jewel-toned rug, was a lovely maiden. Her hair was the color of a raven's wing; her skin pale as ashes. She was so still that, for a moment, Galen feared she wasn't breathing.

Then the princess' eyelids fluttered slightly. Galen knelt at her side, feeling as if he could hardly breathe himself. Seized by a tenderness he had never before experienced, he leaned closer. As soft as a whisper, his lips touched hers.

Book 3

Happily
Ever
After?

15

The Castle Wakes

Galen sat back as the princess drew in a long, ragged breath. Color slowly bloomed in her pale cheeks. Her eyes fluttered, then opened—great pools of deep blue.

For a moment, the two only stared at one another. Then Briar Rose struggled to sit up. "Who are you?" she asked in a puzzled voice. "What are you doing here?"

Galen gently pulled Briar Rose to her feet. "I am Galen of Avondale," he said. "I have rescued you, my lady. You are free at last of Cassandra's curse."

Of course, the king had forbidden anyone to ever speak to Briar Rose of Cassandra's evil gift. So she had no idea what Galen meant. He proceeded to tell her of the curse—and of his quest to save her.

Meanwhile, the rest of the castle filled with sound and activity. For as soon as Galen's kiss wakened Briar Rose, everyone else had also come back to life.

The guards at the gate stared at one another in confusion, then quickly retrieved their swords. The page boys woke also, wondering what they had been talking about when they had been interrupted. Flies began buzzing busily, pigeons took to the air, and the horses neighed and stomped their feet impatiently.

In the throne room, King Walter and Queen Winifred shook off a century of sleep. "What . . . ?" said the king, with a vague sense of disquiet.

"Is something wrong?" asked the queen, who shared her husband's unease.

Just then Briar Rose and Galen came rushing into the room, holding hands. The princess' eyes shone with excitement. "Mother, Father," she said, "this is Galen— and he has saved us all from a dreadful curse."

"Cassandra!" whispered the queen in horror.

Briar Rose stopped in her tracks. "You knew?" Her eyes went to her father. "Both of you knew?"

Her parents nodded and the princess said, "Is she the reason you never allowed me to leave Cambria?"

"Yes," the king said heavily. "I banished spinning wheels and spindles, and we kept you here. We thought we could keep you safe until your sixteenth birthday had come and gone. After that the curse would lose its power."

"But something happened," the queen said. "How did you manage to prick your finger?"

Briar Rose hesitated, a slow blush working its way from cheek to forehead. "I . . . I . . . I guess it was my fault. I went to the tower. When I got there, I found a woman making thread. And—"

"It was Cassandra," the king said.

Briar Rose nodded. "I asked her who she was and what she was doing. She offered to teach me to spin and told me to pick up the spindle. The last thing I recall is pricking my finger. Then—nothing. Until Galen arrived."

She turned to gaze at the prince with shining eyes. "Tell them what you told me," she urged.

So Galen recited the tale of his quest again. When he finished, the queen said, "We owe you a great deal."

"Yes," added the king. "You have saved our beloved daughter and awakened us. Name your reward."

"I need no reward, Your Majesty. All I ask is that you allow me to take your daughter as my bride."

Before the king could answer, Galen turned to Briar Rose. "If you will have me?" he asked softly.

"Of course," answered Briar Rose. For she had loved him as soon as she first looked upon his face.

The king and queen understood at once how it was between the two. They well remembered the feeling, for they had also fallen in love at their first meeting.

"You have our blessing," Walter told Galen.

"Along with our gratitude," added the queen.

Galen looked steadily at the royal couple. "Thank you. But first you should know that even though I am a prince, I am merely the youngest son. I have no kingdom to offer Briar Rose. I can only offer her my heart."

"That is enough for me," said Briar Rose. "I don't care about kingdoms or riches."

"Nor does she need them," commented the king. "This castle and the land around it belong to Briar Rose. That is, unless that has changed as we slept."

Briar Rose hardly heard her father's worried words. Her attention was on Galen. And her thoughts were of the future, not the past.

16

Happiness and Sorrow

And so life returned to Cambria in full force. Soon everyone from the youngest scullery maid to the king and queen was embroiled in wedding preparations. Never had Cambria looked forward to such an event! Cook busied herself baking sweets and roasting meats. The royal seamstress spent her days stitching a silken gown in the deep blue of Briar Rose's eyes. The gardener happily nursed his flowers back into bloom after their long sleep.

As for Briar Rose and Galen, they had eyes only for one another. They spent their days together, talking of the life that lay before them. Galen spoke also of his past, telling Briar Rose every detail of his childhood. "One day I will take you to meet my father and brother," he promised. "They will love you as I do."

However, the prince completely forgot about the warning Miranda had given him about Cassandra. So of that, he said nothing.

Briar Rose was too caught up in her newfound love to think of much else. It took a while before she realized that others weren't quite as happy as she.

One morning, as Effie entered the princess' bedchamber, Briar Rose spotted a tear on her old nurse's cheek. "Why, Effie, what's wrong?" she asked in concern.

Effie wiped the moisture away. "Nothing, Your Majesty. Just a bit of something in my eye, I'm sure," she said quietly. "Now let's get to work. There is much to do before your wedding."

After that, the princess noticed that others around her were prone to long silences. She came across a page boy staring into space with a sad expression on his face. He was so lost in his own thoughts that he never saw her walk by. Crabby old Malcolm seemed strangely subdued. He hardly complained when people tracked mud into the freshly swept courtyard. And once, when Briar Rose went into the kitchen, she found Cook sitting at the table, head in her hands.

The princess also came to realize that her parents were much quieter than normal. And that they smiled less often. One evening she finally asked, "Are you unhappy about my marriage?"

"Of course not," the queen said. "We are very happy for you, Briar Rose. Prince Galen is a wonderful young man."

"He is exactly the kind of person we would have chosen for you," added the king.

"He is wonderful, isn't he?" said Briar Rose, quickly forgetting her concerns. She then went on to list the young prince's many fine qualities.

It was several days later that she overheard a conversation between the king and queen. She had entered the room quietly and found them sitting together by a window. They didn't hear her come in.

"I miss Hugh and William so terribly," the king was saying.

"Yes," said the queen with what sounded like a sob. "I fear their lives were emptier than they should have been."

"It's so hard to know that they lived and died while we slept here," continued the king.

At that, the queen broke down in tears. Her husband put his arms around her, his own eyes glistening.

Briar Rose left without announcing her presence. Her mind was troubled. She certainly hadn't forgotten her brothers. But she realized that she had been half expecting them to ride in from their hunt, laughing and teasing her. Until now, she had avoided the truth—that Hugh and William were gone forever.

And they weren't the only ones. That was what was bothering Effie, she suddenly knew. How could she have been so selfish? So self-centered? Effie's husband and sons hadn't been inside the castle. So they, too, had lived their lives out long ago.

It was the same with Cook, old Malcolm, and the maids, grooms, and page boys. All had wakened to find that someone they loved was lost in the long-ago past.

Still, thought Briar Rose, many of them had traced their families over the century gone by. Just the other day,

Effie had introduced her to a young girl. She had explained that the child was her own great-great-grand-daughter, and that she lived in the village nearby. This was some small consolation, Briar Rose realized, for what had been lost.

But what about her own family? she wondered now. Her parents had never said a word about finding any descendants of Hugh and William. What had happened? Who had been ruling Cambria in her father's absence? And why had none of this occurred to her before?

These questions burned in Briar Rose's mind until she decided she *had* to know the answers. So, leaving Galen on his own for once, she sought out her parents.

"Mother, Father, I must talk to you," the princess said solemnly.

"What is it, dear?" asked the queen.

Briar Rose poured out her questions all in a rush. When she finished, her father sighed. "Sit down," he said, "and we will tell you what we can."

The king went on to explain that within hours of the castle's reawakening, an elderly gentleman had approached the gates. He had requested an audience with the king.

"He said his name was Sir Andrew," the king said. "It turned out that Gregory, my steward, had been his grand-father's grandfather."

The king continued. "You may recall that Sir Gregory was gone the day this all started. He was attending to business in another part of the kingdom."

Briar Rose nodded, remembering the gruff steward who had been so loyal to her father.

The queen took up the story. "Sir Andrew told us that he is the regent of Cambria."

"But to whom was he regent before you awakened, Father?"

"There was no king," replied Walter. "Sir Andrew was managing the kingdom on his own. His father and grandfathers had done the same before him."

"Your brothers set things up that way," the queen explained. "Sir Andrew had documents they had written almost 50 years earlier, when they were both old men. Miranda had assured them that you—and we—could be awakened. And they wanted to keep Cambria intact in case that happened."

"But what about their children and grandchildren?" the princess asked. "Why isn't one of their descendants ruling Cambria? Why haven't we met any members of our family, as everyone else has?"

"It seems that the three of us are the entire family," the queen answered sadly. "Hugh and William never married. They never had children. Apparently they dedicated years to trying to find a way to undo Cassandra's curse. They had to give up eventually. But they arranged things so that Cambria would be waiting if the curse was lifted. They hoped and prayed that that would happen at the end of the 100 years, as Miranda had said it might."

When the queen finished speaking, her husband got

to his feet. He moved heavily to a large chest that sat on a table in the corner of the room. Opening the chest, he removed a rolled-up document.

"You may read this," he said, handing it to Briar Rose.

The princess' eyes filled with tears as she saw the familiar handwriting. She read the letter her brothers had written. In it, they explained that they had appointed their steward as regent, in charge of watching over the kingdom. And that his descendants after him would do the same thing.

Briar Rose's voice quavered as she read the last words aloud. " 'Cambria will wait until the time you awaken, dear Father and Mother. And you as well, our little sister. It is our fondest dream that this will happen. And though we will be gone before that happy day, we trust that you will remember us both with love.' "

"Don't cry, darling," said the queen. "Your brothers loved you very much. They would be so happy to know that you are safe. And that you are to be wed to such a fine young man."

The queen's words were of little consolation to Briar Rose. She fell into her mother's arms, at last sobbing out her sorrow at the loss of her brothers.

"It's all my fault," said Briar Rose later, as she and Galen sat in the rose garden.

"You mustn't blame yourself," Galen comforted her. "The fault is Cassandra's. Her curse is the reason for all the pain you and the others have to bear."

"If I had just stayed in my room," said Briar Rose bitterly. "As I had been told to. My birthday would have come and gone and the curse would have been worthless. None of this would have happened."

Then she stopped, thinking about her words. "But then I wouldn't have found you, Galen," she said breathlessly.

"Nor I you," he returned.

Neither of them could imagine such a thing. Not now that they were together.

"It was supposed to happen, then," said Briar Rose, gazing into her prince's eyes.

"It was fate," replied Galen. "We were meant to be together."

"Forever," added Briar Rose.

17

Cassandra Returns

However, despite her love for Galen, Briar Rose's joy was now tinged with sadness. Feelings of guilt refused to leave her, and she found herself trying to make up for everyone's loss. She constantly asked her parents what they wanted her to do. Then she obeyed every request, no matter how small. She kept her bedchamber unusually neat, leaving little work for the servants. And she drove Effie to distraction, continually asking after the older woman's happiness.

Still, the princess experienced moments of tremendous joy. The more she learned of Galen, the more she loved him. She already knew that he was brave. Otherwise, he never would have dared face Cassandra and the wall of thorns to rescue her. And she knew that he craved adventure and excitement as much as she did. But now she also saw that he was good and kind and gentle. In short, he was all that any princess could ever want in a prince.

Yet there were times when she found herself dissolving in tears for no specific reason. Times like now, when she was by herself in the tower room where it had all begun.

Briar Rose didn't know why she had come to the tower. She hadn't returned to the room since Galen had found her there. But something had made her climb the steps this morning.

Now she sat on a padded stool and stared at the floor. The room was much as she had left it, save for the cobwebs in the corners. Sunlight streamed in through the high, narrow windows. It lit every inch of the tower room, except for the dark shadow cast by the table.

Another tear slipped down the princess' cheek. Impatiently, she dabbed at it with a corner of her gown. "I must stop this nonsense," she said firmly. "I can't go on crying over my mistakes forever."

Suddenly the shadow by the table appeared to shift, then expand. A sound came from that vicinity—almost a chuckle. Then a voice said, "Oh, yes you can, Princess. In fact, you shall weep forever if I have my way."

Briar Rose gasped and jumped to her feet. Cassandra slowly took form from the misty, gray shadow.

"You!" the princess cried. "How dare you come here!"

"How dare I?" echoed Cassandra. "I go wherever I choose, Your Highness. Now, let us return to the matter at hand. Did you think I was going to allow you to live happily ever after? You and your fine prince?"

"Why shouldn't we?" asked Briar Rose angrily. "And

what did I ever do to deserve your curse? I was only a baby. What happened to fill your heart so full of evil?"

"It matters not what was done—or left undone—long ago. All that is behind us now, Princess. What truly matters is that my miserable sister and your equally miserable prince have outwitted my curse. A curse that was meant to punish you and your parents. But there is yet a price to pay. You will never know true happiness, you see."

Then the black-clad woman began to laugh wildly. "If only you were more like me, Briar Rose," she said at last. "I feel no guilt for the pain I cause. That is a punishment you bring upon yourself!

"And it will not be your last punishment, my dear," continued Cassandra. "Oh no, I have other gifts for you. You may have escaped death, but what about your prince? What about your unborn children? What do you think I shall give them when the time is right?"

With that, she swept one arm across her face and whirled in a cloud of smoky gray. In a moment she was gone, leaving behind only the fading sound of her evil laughter.

18

A Difficult Decision

Briar Rose told no one of her meeting with Cassandra. She tried to forget the woman's wicked promises. But in quiet moments, they returned to her. She knew Cassandra had meant every word.

"I have to do something," the princess murmured to herself one evening.

"About what?" asked Galen, who was sitting beside her on a bench in the castle garden.

"Oh, nothing important," replied Briar Rose. Then she fell silent, her mind rejecting idea after idea.

"Rose?" asked Galen. "Are you all right?"

"I'm fine," the princess said. She looked at Galen and willed herself to smile. Then she noticed the chain that hung around his neck and disappeared into his tunic.

"Galen, are you wearing Miranda's medallion?"

"Why, yes." Galen gave the chain a tug, bringing the half heart into view. "I keep it to remind me of you."

"Do you still have the other piece?"

"Yes, here in my bag," the prince answered. He

removed the velvet bag at his waist, opened it, and pulled out the other half of the heart.

Briar Rose studied the broken medallion, her own heart beating wildly. She didn't know why, but something told her Miranda's gift was still important. Perhaps the charm could work its magic again.

"May I have them?" she asked at last. "Please."

Shrugging, Galen removed the medallion from around his neck. "I don't see why not. Their power was for your benefit, after all."

"Thank you," said Briar Rose. She took both pieces of the heart. Then she gave Galen a quick kiss on the cheek and said a hasty good night.

Leaving her prince staring after her, Briar Rose rushed from the garden and up to her bedchamber. Once there, she placed the two pieces of the medallion in the palm of her hand. With the tip of one finger, she pushed the halves together to form a whole.

" 'To save a heart, break a heart,' " she whispered, reading the inscription. "It seems that I have helped to break many hearts. Now if I could just find a way to save them and make them whole."

A single tear fell, splashing onto the jagged line that divided the pieces of the medallion.

"Are you sure you are willing to try?" asked a soft voice behind her.

Briar Rose jumped. Turning, she saw a figure at the other side of the bed. It was a lovely young woman, dressed in a robe that seemed to be made of rainbows and clouds. Her golden hair glowed in the dim light.

"Miranda? Is that who you are?" asked Briar Rose.

"Yes, my dear."

"Can you do it, then? Can you save the hearts I have helped to break?"

"Only you can do that," Miranda answered softly.

"How?"

Instead of answering the princess' question, Miranda asked, "What does the medallion say must be done to save a heart?"

"A heart must be broken," answered Briar Rose.

Miranda repeated what she had said upon her arrival. "Are you sure you are willing to try?"

Suddenly Briar Rose understood. She felt as if part of her had died.

"It's *my* heart that must break, isn't it?" she asked.

Miranda nodded. "Yes, my dear."

"Tell me what I must do," Briar Rose said, fearing that she knew at least part of the answer.

"Cassandra must be destroyed," said Miranda. "At least as she exists in this time."

Briar Rose nodded, then waited for Miranda to continue. She knew there had to be more. And she did not know what was meant by "as she exists in this time."

"Destroying her will not remove the curse, you understand. That was made long ago and in another time. You still have to face it, Briar Rose, but only in that time.

And knowing what you know now, you can prevent the curse from happening again."

"I don't completely understand," the princess admitted when Miranda paused.

"You can try to best Cassandra now. If you succeed, you—and she—and all the others—will be returned to the time before the curse was fulfilled. It will be as if none of this had happened. Then you can make decisions that will protect you and those you love. If you can reach your sixteenth birthday safely, the curse will be powerless."

"And everyone will be happy again. You're sure?"

"None of *them* will remember that any of this happened. So they will be as happy as they ever were."

Briar Rose noted the emphasis Miranda placed on the word *them*. And she suddenly realized what the consequence would be for her. "*I* will remember, won't I? That's why my heart will break. Because I will lose Galen, and yet remember him."

Miranda's silence was all the answer that Briar Rose needed. The princess gazed at the medallion once again, thinking of the young man who had risked his life to save her. And of the pain she would feel each time she thought of him in the future.

"He won't remember me at all?" she asked.

"No, except perhaps as a vague dream."

"That is just as well for him," Briar Rose said, "for I know he truly loves me."

Then the tears started to fall. "What if I don't do it? Isn't there any other way to protect Galen and the children we will one day have?"

"Doing nothing is always a choice," said Miranda. "Perhaps you can find a way to protect those you love. Or perhaps Cassandra will forget her threats."

"But you don't think so, do you?"

Miranda shook her head sadly. "No, my dear. For some reason, my sister's heart is filled with hate. I fear that things will only become worse if she is left unchecked."

Briar Rose wiped her tears away. She knew what she had to do. After all, even if she could find a way to ensure her own happiness with Galen, there was still something else to consider. There was still the pain that others had suffered over losing people they loved. That could only be undone if the curse were never to be fulfilled.

"I'm going to do it," Briar Rose said. "Just tell me how to destroy Cassandra."

"You must solve that part of the problem yourself, I'm afraid," Miranda said. "But I can give you a clue: she is most vulnerable when least visible."

With that, Miranda faded from sight. Briar Rose fell facedown on the bed, sobbing as if her heart were already broken.

19
Waiting

To Briar Rose, the days now raced by. She busied herself preparing for her wedding, knowing it could never happen. Not if she wanted Galen to be safe from Cassandra's evil.

One afternoon as she and Galen walked, she couldn't help asking, "Will you love me forever?"

"Forever and a day," replied Galen with a smile. "You have won my heart, Briar Rose. You have given me yours as well. I shall never give it back."

"And do you promise that you will never forget me?"

"Why would you ask such a question? I couldn't forget you! Besides, we will be together always, finding both adventure and happiness with one another. You will be in my heart and by my side until we are old and gray."

Briar Rose tried to smile, wishing she could look forward to such a thing.

That evening, she had a request for her prince. "I have asked young Sidney to draw your likeness," she told Galen. "If you would pose for him, I'd be most grateful."

"I've heard that the young man has a fine hand with miniatures," Galen replied. "But you have me in the flesh, Briar Rose. Why do you need a portrait?"

The princess pulled a locket from the bag at her waist. "I want to have your picture in here," she said, "so that when we are apart for even a moment, I can look upon your face."

"Very well," said Galen. Soon afterward, he found himself sitting on a stool in his bedchamber. Sidney set to work at once, wondering at the princess' demand that he stop everything else to do this task.

Meanwhile, Briar Rose mulled over the problem of how to fix another meeting with Cassandra. For she had at last determined the meaning of Miranda's words: "She is most vulnerable when least visible." It had taken her some time, but she had finally realized that there were times when Cassandra was present, yet not visible. It was when she took the form of a gray, swirling mist. Therefore, that had to be when she could be destroyed.

But for days, the princess saw no sign of Cassandra. Briar Rose checked every shadowy corner but saw no dark, misty cloud as evidence of an evil presence. She even talked to herself in her bedchamber, saying things such as, "She doesn't frighten me" and "She would never dare hurt Galen!"

However, if she had hoped to enrage Cassandra and cause her to appear, she failed miserably.

Finally Briar Rose decided to ask her parents more about the curse. Why had Cassandra been so angry? What had happened to make her give such a terrible gift to a tiny baby?

"We chose not to invite her to your naming-day celebration," sighed the queen. "That is all it was."

"Why was she not invited?"

"We knew her heart was black. She had put a spell on a young man at William's naming day," the queen explained. "We didn't want her upsetting things at yours as well."

"But she did anyway," said Briar Rose sadly.

Still, her mother's words gave the princess an idea. If not being invited to a royal celebration had infuriated Cassandra once, maybe it would do so again. And if she were angry, surely she would appear to say so.

So the princess threw herself into the wedding preparations with enthusiasm. And when the guest list was drawn up, Cassandra, of course, was not included.

The day finally arrived when messengers went forth to invite everyone near and far. Briar Rose went back to the tower for the first time in weeks. There, she stood at the window and looked out. Her fingers played with the locket around her neck—which now cradled a tiny image of Galen.

"At least Cassandra won't be at my wedding," she said in clear tones. "She won't be able to ruin that day for me."

Cautiously, Briar Rose peered around the room. Was that a patch of mist by the table? No, it was only a shadow.

An hour later, the discouraged princess went downstairs. What was she going to do if she couldn't lure Cassandra into becoming partly visible? How could she destroy Cassandra if she never saw her again?

20

Into the Flames

The day had finally arrived—the day that Briar Rose and Galen were to wed.

In her bedchamber, the princess fidgeted nervously. "Heavens, my girl, whatever is the matter with you?" asked Effie, who was trying to arrange Briar Rose's long, curly hair. "I can't take care of these tangles if you won't stand still."

"I'm sorry, Effie," said Briar Rose. But a moment later, she was fidgeting again.

"You're not having second thoughts about marrying Prince Galen, now, are you?" asked Effie with concern.

"Of course not," replied Briar Rose. "I love him more than life itself, Effie. You know that."

"As you should. He is a fine young man, even if he does encourage your talk of adventure. As if you need to leave Cambria and visit Avondale," Effie huffed.

"Now hold still and let me get on with your hair, so we can have this wedding," she continued. "It's high time people had something happy to think about."

"Are you still so very unhappy, then?" asked Briar Rose softly. She twisted her head around to watch Effie's face.

Effie dropped the brush, giving up for the moment. "No, Your Majesty, I'm not exactly unhappy. I just can't help missing the ones I left behind, that's all. I know you feel the same way. After all, your own two brothers . . ."

Effie's voice trailed off for a moment; then she picked up the brush again. "But let's just move on with our lives, shall we?" she said in no-nonsense tones. "There is no point in moaning about things we cannot control." Briar Rose winced as the brush once again swept through her tangled curls.

While Effie worked, the princess thought back to the last few weeks. She had been counting on Cassandra showing up once word of the wedding date went out. She had been sure the evil woman would appear to protest the fact that she hadn't been invited.

But that had probably been a silly idea, Briar Rose thought now. After all, why would Cassandra expect to be invited after all the evil she had done?

"There," said Effie softly. When Briar Rose looked up, she saw that her old nurse had tears in her eyes. "What a beautiful bride you are."

Briar Rose truly did look lovely. Her silk gown was the same sapphire blue as her eyes. Intricate lace edged the neck and sleeves, and a long lace-trimmed train spread out behind. The golden circlet her mother had worn at her own wedding now gleamed atop Briar Rose's curls.

"It's almost time to head downstairs, dear. Your guests are all here. And your prince is waiting for you."

"I know," said Briar Rose. Then she threw her arms around the older woman. "Thank you for always being here for me. You know I love you so, Effie."

"And I you, child," replied the nurse. "Now, if you'll just give me a moment to pull myself together," she said, dabbing at her wet cheeks. Effie left the room hurriedly, hardly bothering to disguise a loud sniff.

After her nurse left, Briar Rose gazed in the mirror. This should be the happiest day of my life, she thought. Yet I feel as if there is a dark cloud hanging over it.

Suddenly she noticed that there *was* a cloud of sorts. Not over her head, but in the far corner of the room, reflected in the mirror.

"Cassandra!" she cried, turning in that direction.

The mist seethed, then seemed to solidify. In seconds, it took the form of the black-robed woman.

"A touching scene," sneered Cassandra. "And it won't be the last bout of tears for those you love."

"Why are you doing this?" cried Briar Rose.

"Why?" echoed Cassandra. "Perhaps because I want to, my dear. Perhaps to pay you back for my own misery—you and all the other happy souls in this kingdom."

"But no one here has caused you any real pain,"

protested Briar Rose. "Surely not the kind of misery you have caused for us."

"That is for me to judge, Your Majesty. And my judgment is that you shall pay the price for your parents' lack of respect."

With that, Cassandra gave her usual evil laugh. Her body began to shimmer, then dissolved back into a misty cloud. Slowly the gray cloud rose from the floor.

Horrified, Briar Rose realized that she had to act immediately. Dashing to the table, she seized the small golden chest that held her jewelry and dumped out the contents.

Then, opening the lid as far as it would go, she hurried forward.

The cloud of mist swirled madly around Briar Rose. It was as cold as winter, with icy fingers that seemed to grasp her greedily. Then it began to collect into one dark cloud, as if Cassandra were preparing to take human form again.

Shivering from both cold and fear, the princess clapped the chest shut around the cloud, trapping it inside. The box began to vibrate so wildly that she could barely hold onto it. Then Cassandra's laugh, muffled by the walls of the small chest, sounded from within.

Holding the chest against her to prevent Cassandra's escape, Briar Rose looked around desperately. It was clear that trapping the evil woman wasn't enough. How could she destroy her?

The princess' eyes lit on the fire that burned brightly in one corner. Surely even Cassandra couldn't survive that! With all her strength, Briar Rose hurled the chest and its contents into the fireplace.

The flames turned black and bubbled like burning tar. A terrible howling sound full of anger and hate rose from the fireplace. It roared through the room as if seeking an escape route. For a moment, Briar Rose feared that Cassandra's evil spirit was going to survive.

There was a flash of bright light from the hearth, and then—silence.

Briar Rose collapsed onto her bed in a faint.

21

Undone!

Briar Rose sighed and rolled over. Pinpricks of light teased her eyelids. Surely it wasn't morning already, she thought. She opened her eyes reluctantly.

Sitting up, the princess gazed around the familiar candlelit room, trying to recall her dream.

Then she remembered.

Cassandra! Had the evil woman been destroyed?

The curse! Could it be prevented from happening?

Briar Rose tumbled off the bed. She half ran to the door and yanked it open.

"Goodness, child, what is your hurry?" asked Effie, who had been just about to enter.

"Oh, Effie!" cried Briar Rose, throwing her arms around the older woman.

"Whatever is the matter, my dear?" replied the nurse. "As if I didn't know," she continued. "You're upset about having to stay in your chambers, aren't you? Trust me, Briar Rose, your parents have their reasons for asking you not to leave."

"What day is it, Effie?" demanded the princess.

"What day? Why it's Tuesday evening, child. And tomorrow is your birthday. You know that. There is going to be such a wonderful celebration in your honor. Sixteen! I cannot tell you how happy I am to see this day arrive. As is everyone who loves you."

"What about Hugh and William?" asked the princess. "Are they here?"

"They are due back at any moment," Effie replied. "I'll send them up as soon as they arrive, if you want. I know they will have some tales to tell you."

"Yes, yes, of course they will," murmured the princess.

Effie kissed Briar Rose on the cheek. "Good evening, love," she said softly. Then she bustled off.

Briar Rose sank down on her bed. She had done it! It was as if she had never pricked her finger. Never helped to fulfill Cassandra's wicked curse.

Or had it all just been a dream? she wondered. Had none of it ever really happened? Had she just had an awful nightmare?

One hand went to her neck. A golden chain lay there, cool against her skin. An oval locket hung from it.

Trembling, Briar Rose opened the locket. A familiar face gazed up at her. It was Galen.

It *had* happened. All of it. She had found her prince— and lost him.

Fighting back tears, Briar Rose closed the locket. "I will never forget you, Galen," she whispered, "though I know you won't remember me."

Then she sat down to read and pass the time until she could go to bed. She would not leave her chamber this evening, no matter how strong the temptation. For she knew what waited for her in the tower room.

"You are going to be disappointed, Cassandra," Briar Rose whispered later that evening. She was lying in bed, unable to sleep. And then, at the stroke of midnight, she heard a horrible, angry cry. It came from high in the westernmost part of the castle.

"A wish for happiness," announced King Walter the next day. He smiled in his daughter's direction.

"Happiness!" echoed the party guests.

Briar Rose looked around the great room. It was filled with people, from lords and ladies to commoners and village folk. There were her parents, happier than she ever remembered them. There was Effie, beaming with pride and standing with her husband and sons, who were excited to be part of the festivities. And there were her brothers, strong and real and full of life.

As music and excited voices swirled around her, Briar Rose thought about the future. Almost 100 years from now a young prince would leave home to seek adventure.

What would Galen find? she wondered.

Enough adventure to keep him content, she hoped. But more importantly, she wanted him to find happiness.

As I will one day too, Briar Rose told herself.

Though I will never forget Galen.

Then she settled back to enjoy the celebration. She had already received her most precious gift, she knew. The gift of being loved—both by those who surrounded her here, and by a young prince who had yet to be born.

With a smile, she turned her attention to her guests.

22

100 Years Later

Prince Galen removed his plumed hat and scratched his head. His dark eyes studied the crossroads ahead.

"Where now, Micah?" he asked. "Cambria is a huge place. It is hard to know exactly where to go."

The handsome young prince had arrived in the kingdom only the day before. It had been a long, hard trip through the mountains that formed Cambria's eastern boundary. Still, something had driven him onward. After telling his father, King Frederick of Avondale, that he was going to seek adventure, he could hardly return home without a tale or two to tell. And certainly nothing that had happened to him yet would be worthy of a troubadour's tune.

The early morning sun warmed his back and lit the hard-packed road that stretched off to the west. Other roads, obviously less traveled, led to the north and south.

The prince's horse snorted, then pranced forward a few feet. "West, Micah? Is that your choice?" asked Galen with a laugh. "Very well, then. You've convinced me."

With that, the prince tapped his heels against his horse's sides. Moving as one, they headed west.

Galen wasn't entirely sure why he had been so set on reaching Cambria. True, even in tiny Avondale, he had heard tales of the kingdom. It was said to be a peaceful land, with three fine castles. Each was ruled over by the descendants of one of the children of a much-loved king and queen who had lived a century before. Together, they worked to protect and care for their subjects. The description had hardly been of a place that would hold the excitement and adventure that Galen was seeking.

Still, it was here he had come. Now he rode beside well-tended fields and through small, bustling villages. Everywhere he was greeted with hospitality and interest.

"Would you care for a drink of cool water, my lord?" asked an old woman when Galen stopped by a stone well.

He nodded, then drank gratefully, rinsing the dust of the road from his throat. "Thank you, good woman," he said as he handed back the dipper.

"You're most welcome, sir," she responded, "to the water and to Cambria."

"It is a fine place," said Galen as he gazed around the village. "Is all your kingdom this prosperous?"

"Aye, sir. The land is rich and the crops seem to grow faster than they can be harvested."

Staring at Galen with curiosity, the old woman asked, "And where might you be headed, my lord?"

Galen smiled. "I have no set destination, madam. I am just interested in seeing your country."

"Well, being that you're a noble, I'd suggest you continue west," the old woman said. "Within a day's journey you'll reach our largest and finest castle. The royal family is all there now, come together from other parts of the kingdom. So there is much going on. I'm sure you would be a welcome guest."

"Perhaps I will do that," murmured Galen. Thanking the woman once more, he mounted Micah. Then, suddenly curious, he leaned down to ask, "Why has everyone come to the one castle?"

"Ah, our princess is turning 16," said the woman. "There's to be a great celebration."

"I see," said Galen thoughtfully. Then he and Micah set off to the west.

By the middle of the next day, Galen found himself riding through a pleasant forest. Broad oaks shaded the road from the bright sunshine, their leaves washed clean of dust by the rain that had fallen the night before. Birds sang noisily overhead, and forest creatures skittered through the underbrush. Other than that, and the clip-clop of Micah's feet, the woods were silent.

That silence was broken by the sound of thundering hooves. The noise came from the right, as if someone were galloping at full speed.

Suddenly a horse and its rider burst through the trees

directly behind Galen. Micah reared in alarm, unseating his rider. Galen slid to the ground, landing facedown in a muddy spot beside the road.

The other horse skidded to a stop, just missing the fallen prince. It stood there, breathing heavily and pawing the ground. In seconds, its rider had dismounted.

"My apologies, sir," a light voice said.

Galen got to his feet and wiped mud from his eyes. He was prepared to give the lad a piece of his mind. However, when he turned, the angry words died on his lips. This was no reckless lad before him. Instead, it was a young woman. A beautiful girl with flowing hair the red-gold of a summer sunset and blue eyes that shimmered with laughter.

She was laughing at him, Galen realized. And with good reason. His hat hung over one ear and his face was covered with mud.

He righted his hat, still staring at the girl. His heart hammered in his chest—surely she could see it beating there! He had never seen anyone so beautiful. So alive.

Galen had found his great adventure. He had fallen in love with this girl—without even knowing her name.

At Galen's silence, the expression in the girl's eyes turned from laughter to concern. "Are you hurt, sir? Shall I ride for help?"

At last he found his voice, "No, miss, I am fine," he said. "Just a bit embarrassed."

"I'm the one who should be embarrassed," she admitted. "Mother is always telling me I must learn to ride like a lady. But it's just so boring to do so!"

At that, Galen had to laugh. He bowed, saying, "Well, my lady, I can see that you are anything but boring. And I must confess that I understand your need to ride like the wind. I am the same way myself."

"Thank you, kind sir," the girl said with a hasty curtsy. Then she looked at him with interest. "I wish others understood that feeling as well. And now, the least I can do is offer you the hospitality of the castle, where you can get cleaned up. Come, I will show you the way."

The castle? thought Galen. But he had no chance to ask any questions. The girl had already mounted her horse and headed into the woods. Hoisting himself onto Micah, Galen followed.

Twenty minutes later, the woods opened into a broad, sunny meadow. A magnificent stone castle stood at the far side. The girl kicked her horse's sides and began to move even faster. She galloped to the castle gate, where she dismounted and waited for Galen.

"Come," she said impatiently. Then, nodding to the guards, she led Galen over the drawbridge and into a wide courtyard.

Galen followed as if in a trance. Through the courtyard, up the steps, and into a huge hall.

"Briar Rose!" someone called out. "I have been searching high and low for you!"

A plump woman was bearing down on them, her forehead creased with worry. "You must get dressed. It is almost time for your party to begin."

"I know, Mabel, I know," Briar Rose said. "And I've brought another guest."

Mabel turned to study Galen. "Hmmph," she said, planting her hands on her hips. "Where did you find this one, Your Majesty?"

Galen's head was spinning. A princess! He had fallen in love with Cambria's princess. Suddenly remembering his manners, he bowed to the older woman. "Excuse me, madam," he said. "I am Prince Galen of Avondale."

"Prince?" said Mabel. "You hardly look the part, sir."

Briar Rose interrupted. "That is my fault, Mabel. I spooked his horse. So now if you could see that he is offered soap and water—and some clean clothes, I will go and get dressed myself."

With that, she smiled prettily at Galen. "I look forward to seeing you at the banquet, sir. It is my birthday today, you see." In a flurry of skirts, she was gone.

Fifteen minutes later, Galen gazed around the bedchamber to which a young serving girl had escorted him. Rich tapestries hung on the walls, and the furniture gleamed from years of polishing. But the prince's thoughts weren't on his surroundings. They were on the princess. She was the most enchanting girl he had ever seen. But why would she be interested in a penniless prince? he thought in disgust. A younger son with absolutely nothing to inherit? Briar Rose of Cambria was obviously a girl who could have any prince she chose.

He gave his image a quick check in the mirror. The borrowed clothing fit him well, he noted with relief. And certainly he looked more presentable with the mud cleaned from his face.

There was a knock on the door and Mabel entered. "Hmmph!" she said, crossing her arms on her chest. "At least you appear decent enough now to attend the princess' birthday party, young man. Come, I will show you the way to the banquet hall."

Galen followed Mabel, who complained all the way

down the curving stairway. "The princess has been running wild lately," she said, "as if she doesn't want to grow up. All she talks about is seeking adventure. And, if she has her way, she'll seek it outside the castle walls."

Underneath the complaints, Galen could hear the woman's love for her charge. And he felt a growing kinship with this spirited princess. For she, too, clearly valued adventure more than quiet contentment.

They entered a large room lit with hundreds of candles. There were dozens of guests, and it took Galen a while to find Briar Rose. But at last he spotted her, looking even more beautiful than before in a gown of sea-green silk. An attractive couple sat nearby, gazing at the princess fondly. The king and queen, Galen was sure. Taking a deep breath, he headed in that direction.

Briar Rose was occupied with one of her guests, so Galen bowed to the royal couple. He said, "Your Majesties, I am Prince Galen of Avondale. I bring you greetings from my father, King Frederick."

"Ah, Prince Galen," said the king in a friendly fashion. "You are the unfortunate young man our daughter managed to unseat from his horse. Our apologies on her behalf."

"Yes," added the queen. "And you are most welcome. We have heard of your father and are glad you are able to visit Cambria in his place."

The formalities over, Galen turned toward the

princess. Briar Rose was now talking to a young man who seemed to hang on her every word. To Galen's relief, the princess finally dismissed her admirer.

Quickly, Galen stepped forward and bent over her hand. "Happy birthday, Princess," he murmured.

"Ah, the gallant horseman," laughed Briar Rose.

As Galen raised his eyes to the princess' face, her laughter died. Her cheeks paled and her eyes darkened.

"Your Majesty," said Galen, "what is wrong? Have I offended you somehow?"

"No, no, of course not," replied Briar Rose in a voice that trembled a bit. "It's only that for a moment, with the mud off your face, you seemed very familiar."

Galen noticed that the princess' hand went to the locket she wore around her neck. Then she looked at him again, smiled, and turned to the next well-wisher.

The prince found himself caught up in the festivities. He never had another chance to speak to the princess. So it was the next morning before the two came face-to-face again, in the castle garden.

"Good day, Your Highness," Galen said, bowing.

"Er . . . good day, my lord," replied Briar Rose. "I trust you slept well."

She seemed far less sure of herself than at their first meeting, Galen noted. "Have I upset you in some way, my lady?" Galen asked. He prayed that he had not done so, for he could not bear the thought.

Startled, Briar Rose said, "Oh no. It is just that . . ." Again, she hesitated. Then she motioned to a stone bench beside the garden path. "Please sit down."

Galen took a seat next to the princess, who was silent for a time. Then she said, "I told you that you seemed familiar, Prince Galen. This is why." She opened the locket she wore around her neck and held it for Galen to see. He peered at the faded image that was framed there.

His own face stared up at him.

"Hmmm," the prince murmured, not sure how to respond. "A remarkable likeness. Who is the young man?"

"I don't know," admitted Briar Rose. "This necklace belonged to my grandmother's grandmother. I was named for her, actually. She had said that no one was to bear her name except the first princess to be born in my generation. And that princess was to receive both her name and this locket."

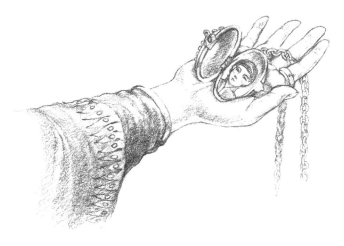

"Do you know anything else about the other Briar Rose?" asked Galen with interest. Looking into her eyes, he felt a tug of something both long forgotten and yet to come. But the feeling quickly faded.

"Oh, I've heard all the stories about her," the princess said. "She was known as a good and kind queen who cared deeply for her subjects." Briar Rose gave Galen a crooked smile. "For that reason, bearing her name is a great honor, but one that I find hard to live up to."

"I am sure you are worthy of the name."

The princess looked into his eyes for several heartbeats, then nodded. "Thank you. I hope so."

Then she went on with her account. "According to family legend, there was always something a bit sad about Briar Rose. Although she did marry a good man, it was said that he was her second love. That her heart had been badly broken when she was a young girl."

The princess paused and studied the image in the locket. "I have always wondered if this young man was the reason for her sadness," she said. Then she snapped the locket shut and turned her attention to Galen.

"Now, tell me about yourself," she said.

The two began to talk, soon discovering that there was much they wanted to learn about one another.

That conversation was only the beginning for Briar Rose and Galen. Before long, the princess had fallen as much in love with him as he had with her. All of Cambria was soon caught up in the joy of planning a royal wedding.

When that day arrived, the castle was crowded. Everyone who was anyone had come to wish the young couple long lives filled with love and happiness.

Midway through the festivities, an excited guard burst noisily into the great hall. Conversations ceased as everyone turned to see what he was shouting about.

"The roses!" the guard cried. "The roses!"

"What about them?" asked the king impatiently. "What is so important that you must interrupt us?"

"They are in bloom, sire," the guard explained. "I was just standing there, as usual. And suddenly the bushes began to flower."

The wedding couple and their guests swarmed into the courtyard to see for themselves. The ancient bushes stood at either side of the castle gate. For as long as anyone could remember, they had been nothing but leaves and thorny branches. But now the air was filled with the heavy, sweet scent of the hundreds of white blossoms that covered each bush.

The roses bloomed for weeks, welcoming all who entered the castle courtyard. Then, as roses do, they shed their petals. For a few days, they formed a sweet-smelling carpet underfoot. Then the petals dried up and blew away on the late-summer breezes.

However, the next June, the roses burst into bloom

again, just as magnificently as they had the year before. They continued to bloom every June thereafter. It was as if the grand old bushes had decided to celebrate each anniversary of the date that Briar Rose and her prince began to live happily ever after.